Ghost Writers 2
A Collection of
Halloween Stories

by

Lago Vista Writers Group

For Information, address
rseibert@advancedconceptdesign.com
axlerod@peoplepc.com
e- print September 2025 ISBN 13:978-1-965535-18-9
Paperback October 2025 ISBN 13 978-1-965535-19-6
Printed in the United States of America

Contents

The Garden of Webs

by Derek Day

The summer of 1959 was blistering in west Texas. Heat shimmered off the cracked earth as Ray worked under his father's watchful eye. His father was a strict man, but fair, and he believed in teaching his son to respect the land.

One afternoon, as Ray gathered ripe tomatoes, he carelessly swiped at a large spider web glistening between two stalks. His father, sitting on the porch, caught the act and called him over. That evening, by lantern light, his father explained that the spider was an Orb Weaver—a silent guardian of the garden. "They eat the insects that would eat our food," his father said. "You leave them be. They're part of the balance."

Ray listened, and something inside him changed.

The next day, he caught a grasshopper and tossed it into the web. He watched in fascination as the spider darted out, wrapping the prey in silk, draining it dry. From then on, feeding the Orb Weavers became a ritual. He came to know them by their patterns, their habits, even the way their webs shimmered in moonlight. Some spiders grew so accustomed to his presence that they seemed to wait for him.

Seasons of the Web

Years turned into decades. Ray's father passed on, but the gardens lived in Ray's blood. He grew food, sold at markets, and started community plots. He never earned much, but his joy was in the soil and in the silken threads strung like jewels between his rows.

The Orb Weavers multiplied, generation after generation, as if bound to Ray's life. Some of them were twenty or more generations descended from those first webs his father told him to respect. They seemed to rely on him, waiting for their gifts of grasshoppers and beetles.

Ray was never alone in the garden.

The Sickness

The Texas sun, his lifelong companion, turned on him. Decades of exposure carved melanoma into his skin. By 2025, lesions marred his face and shoulders. He endured hospital visits, scalpels carving away chunks of flesh, the stink of antiseptic replacing the earthy perfume of his garden.

That summer was mercifully mild, but Ray's strength waned. The garden grew wild.

The spiders waited, hungry, their webs sagging with neglect. Some starved, their curled husks clinging to dead vines.

The Offering

When autumn came, Ray's wife left for Dallas to visit the grandchildren. Alone, Ray hobbled into his garden, shocked by the ruin—shriveling crops, brown leaves, sagging vines. But in the center, something extraordinary caught his eye.

The Orb Weavers had woven together a single colossal web. It stretched across the garden like a cathedral window, silken and shimmering, anchored to the earth and sky alike.

As he drew closer, he realized the spiders were watching. Hundreds of them, their bodies fat and glistening, their legs twitching in eerie unison. The air vibrated with their quiet hunger.

At the base of the web, nestled like an offering, grew a massive pumpkin, perfect and orange, thriving against all odds. Ray bent to harvest it—his last gift from the soil.

But as he reached forward, his arm snagged the web. The silk clung tight, impossibly strong. He tugged, but the strands only tightened, pulling him deeper.

The Feast

The spiders moved.

From the edges of the great web, they descended in swarms—hundreds, maybe thousands. They rushed over him in a tide of bristling legs, fangs clicking like a chorus of knives. Ray screamed, but the sound was muffled as silk threads wrapped around his mouth, his chest, his limbs.

He had watched them feed a thousand times. Now he understood what the grasshoppers felt.

They pierced his flesh with needle-fangs, injecting venom that burned and numbed at once. His skin turned cold as his veins filled with poison. He convulsed, struggling, but the silk tightened until bones cracked beneath the pressure.

Dozens of them worked in frantic unity, wrapping him in layer after layer. His eyes bulged as they covered his face, leaving only a trembling cocoon where he once stood. Inside, Ray felt his blood pulled out in steady pulses, his muscles dissolving into broth. He was being emptied, drained alive, every twitch of their fangs tearing at his nerves until pain gave way to blackness.

Hours later, the cocoon sagged, dripping with what had been Ray. By morning, only a husk remained, gnawed to bone.

The Whispering Web

When his wife returned a week later, she found the garden eerily quiet.

The pumpkin still sat unclaimed, but at the center of the monstrous web hung her husband's skeleton, bleached and stripped clean, silk strands clinging to hollow sockets.

She screamed, but the garden only echoed with whispers—the dry hiss of spider legs across silk. And sometimes, when the wind rustled the web, she swore she could hear Ray's voice, calling softly from within the threads.

The Orb Weavers had kept their guardian.

Forever.

The Elevator Story

by Devane Clarke

For Hitch

My wife and I got on a crowded elevator at the fifth floor. I said to her, "Without a doubt it was the most gruesome sight I have ever seen. There was blood everywhere. Body parts were scattered around the room."

I ignored the inquisitive glances as we passed the fourth floor. "It's hard to believe. Three people are dead, and the cops won't do a damn thing."

The bell chimed for the third floor. "So, I told him, lycanthropy is a dangerous affliction. You should probably get professional help."

No one got off on the second floor. "You wouldn't believe what he said to me."

The passengers were breathless as the door opened and we exited the elevator on the first floor. As we walked away my wife asked, "So, what did he say?"

"Well, nothing really," I replied, "that's just my elevator story."

"The Elevator Story" was originally published in *Intangience Magazine*, copyright 2023, HeartString Publishing.

Bringers of the Light

by Anna Jean Seibert

In a far-flung edge of the old Roman Empire in a place called Britain, there was a family who were "crofters", that meant they had sheep and chickens and ducks and all kinds of animals that lived in the area under their house. In this cold climate, a family living with and above their animals stayed warm better than those who couldn't. In the summer, the sheep were taken up to the hills where it was cool and the wool then grew heavier than those who had grazed down on the plains. Then in the fall, whoever was the family shepherd had to bring them down to winter ground.

So, on this October day, Alex, the 11 year old son, was sent to bring the sheep down. He hated to do this alone; always before his older brother was with him. But Beck was needed somewhere else, and so he went up the path alone. He could see across the valley and noticed movement. Many movements among the trees seemed to be men in white robes and so he realized it must be near the fall solstice that was a high holy day for the druids, who still lived there among them. His own family had adopted the new Christian faith. His mother was very devout. As he and his dog rounded up the sheep, he noticed it was surely getting dark, and he wanted to hurry, but sheep cannot be hurried.

He began to see shadowy movements in the trees, and he hoped they were druids and not wolves. Were they white or were they Gray? He couldn't fight any wolves, not he and his dog and as he came down lower and lower it became darker and darker, and he was more and more afraid.

He really got frightened. As he tried to peer deepest further into the woods, he noticed a faint light bobbing through the shadows. He was so grateful he almost cried. Whoever was carrying a light wasn't a wolf. The figure broke free of the forest and came up the trail carrying two gourd lanterns. "Oh, thank goodness the light will keep the wolves back if they are wolves."

As the figure came close, Alex recognized his mother. She had come to find him as it got dark. She knew he would need a light.

When they arrived home, and he was getting the sheep into their, pen his brother joined him. "I'll bet you were glad for all our mother's prayers for you tonight."

"Yes. Of course, but I was even more grateful for the sight of her bringing me the lights."

Jackalope

by Raymond Walter Seibert

Geneva Switzerland:

Down the hall from the Hadron Collider where the search for the "God Particle" is in progress, the genetics laboratory of Dr, Hans Grubner is working late.

From various viles in his storage, Dr. Grubner pulls, "the telepathic ability of ants to work in unison, the vicious nature of the wolverine, the butting instinct of the mountain rams, the sharp prong horns and muscular strength of the antelope." Dr. Grubner comes to a microscope and inserts the genetics into the egg and ovum of a baby jackrabbit. "Put these genetics into a jack, I think I will call it a Jackalope, Ha, Ha, Ha, Ha."

Some time later, a vicious chewing sound is followed by a banging, as an unholy form streaks down the hall and into the Hadron Collider itself.

"This run should do it," Dr. Ruby Stone beamed a smile at her colleagues.

"The New York Times reports that there are twelve-thousand or more people that believe that we are building a door for the devil." Dr. Otto Uberman chuckled.

We will detect the God Particle today," Dr. Stone affirmed. The Collider hummed as unimaginable forces smashed into infinity infinitesimal particles of matter. "We've done it," Ruby yelled. "We've got the data. We see the Higgs Boson." The run was completed, the hum ceased. The God Particle had at last been found.

Astonished faces freeze on each scientist as a fleeting form flees from the Hadron Collider tube and out the door. "What in God's name was that?" Dr. Ruby Stone whispers. No one answers as only she saw the Jackalope. All the others will not admit to what they saw.

Down the hall the Jackalope flees, setting off alarms. Security doors slam shut. A security guard, hearing the alarms, opens the outside gate and steps out to try and look for the trouble as a strange form streaks through the door and into the outside world. The genetics of Jackalope are loose.

The first time I saw a Jackalope, I was deer hunting on my father's ranch land in Texas just west of the nuclear power station north of Glen Rose. Squaw Creek Nuclear Power Station stood in the background in the far distance like two giant tits. I had placed a salt lick on a deer trail right between the two tits, seen from where I was hidden with my thirty-thirty.

This rather oversized rabbit, with horns, came to the mineral salts for a lick. A red fox came out of some bushes to my right running at the rabbit. Quicker than the eye can follow, the rabbit met the fox head on. The rabbit stabbed the fox through the eyes and into the brain. I stayed very still as this creature examined its kill in a most un-rabbit like manner.

After this, as I now called it, 'Jackalope' departed. I picked up the fox and took it back to the ranch house, where we examined it totally. "Dad," I said, "you are not going to believe this one."

"Well, what happened." He questioned.

The first Jackalope that I killed was in October in twenty-twenty-four. I had been out hunting all day with my father's German Lugar that he had acquired from his brother, along with some ammunition. I had blown an armadillo to smithereens. I shot a vulture out of the air. My blood lust for the day not slaked, I decided to trade the Luger for a twenty-two-two-forty telescopic rifle.

I would have been alright, if I had saddled Lady, she wasn't gun shy. I forgot that King was, sometimes. Jackalopes were common, but not thick like now. They were very hard to hit, almost quicker than the bullet. That's why I had the twenty-two-two-forty telescopic rifle for the high muzzle velocity rather than the bigger more cumbersome and slower bullet of the thirty-ought-six. I lined up the cross hairs on a big one, not far away, right on his neck, and squeezed the trigger really slow. King spooked when the gun went off.

King got the bit between his teeth and overpowered me. I couldn't jerk it loose. He ran a mile over the front cattle guard and turned into a lot of mobile home sales. The lot was stacked full of mobile homes in long lines with the windows rolled out almost touching. King ran between two lines of mobile homes with the windows rolled out on both sides. Edges of windows zipped by on either side of my neck for several trailer lengths and then about mid midway down the long line, King just stopped. I got off careful to avoid an edge and found a place to turn him around, now acting perfectly normal except the twitching of his eyes which told me he was expecting me to use the reins on his face as someone must have done to him in his past. I was just glad to be alive and unhurt. After I stopped shaking, I walked him back to where I had thrown the rife down while holding on for dear life.

Walked King back to the dead Jackalope, he was skittish and shied away from the weird looking creature, which suddenly twitched like it was coming back to life, so I put two more rounds in its head to make sure, even though the first shot had been right through the neck. I had the head taxidermized and it was on the wall at the ranch house until the Jackalopes began to congregate and threaten to break the windows. Safter that we took it down, where it couldn't be seen from the outside. Of course, today, you wouldn't think about going outside without an automatic an several clips. You wouldn't last. You'd be attacked and overwhelmed in minutes.

The first time I was attacked by a group of Jackalopes was about a month ago. I wasn't prepared. Now we are arming ourselves against the onslaught.

Later with the flying robots named after Fudd (Flying Ubicates Demolition Devices), we began to thin them out a little. There were sections of some of the counties that were almost Jackalope free. Still, you never knew, the herds could move quickly, overwhelming a garden and pasture overnight.

They treed me that first attack and I climbed a tree. But they can jump high and once on a limb can jump from limb to limb. I had a good walking stick that I always carried on a walk and had tough work to keep them knocked off. I had a good fight on my hands and they kept me there for two days and then suddenly moved on.

Without the Jackalope killing robots, we wouldn't have had a chance and would have been overwhelmed. The first Elmer Fudd #1 we called him, just rolled out with twelve-gauge buckshot. Later FUDD's could target and kill up to twelve Jackalopes per second. Still, in coordinated attacks, the FUDDs were overwhelmed and dismantled, as if the Jackalopes were trying to know how to control them through telepathic radio waves, ultrasound, maybe like bats. No doubt they were evolving new skills for the progressing warfare. The Jackalopes were purposely looking for something in the integrated wiring auto control circuits. Dad was killed by a FUDD that was turned back on us the day that they began the attack on the Squaw Creek Reactor.

We are making a last stand, and they keep swarming in butting against the vessel containment walls, sensing the forty-year-old radiated concrete is weakened. They are expected to breach the containment and reach the core by tomorrow evening, and the Fort-Worth-Dallas Metroplex has been

ordcred into an emergency evacuation order. Strang, it's Halloween.

God Help Us the reactor is reported

going critical,,,,,,,,,,,,,,,,,,,,,,,

Rachel: The Bone Garden

by Derek Day

Chapter One — Softness With Teeth

The house leaned like a drunk on a lamppost. Every floorboard had a groan in it, every wall a stain, every window a smear that never wiped clean. Rachel kept the lights dim because bright bulbs showed too much truth: the dust constellations, the rust in the sink, the listless sag in her shoulders.

She told herself she was fine. She fed the kittens like saints receive communion, careful and reverent, whispering their names like prayers...Friday, Saturday, Sunday,

Vladimir, Madge and Robert.. Their purrs filled the rooms like a motor humming in a chest cavity. She loved the gentleness of them, the warm bread-smell of their fur, the tiny paws kneading her throat as she dozed with the TV hissing blue.

But nights were long and she had a way of sliding off the edge of herself. When the Rum pulled the trapdoor, she'd stare into the kitchen window where her reflection floated behind grease and night. It wasn't just her face. It was a mask of her face, like someone had pressed a Rachel-shaped stamp into the dark.

"Talk to me," she said, smoke hooking her lip. "Tell me I'm not a ghost that does the dishes."

The reflection smiled with teeth that were a fraction too sharp. The smile said: You were meant for more than this. Meant for blood, not bleach.

Outside, the alley coughed up a siren and the cats lifted their heads. One by one they turned toward the window, ears like arrowheads. The air got tight and hot. The bulb above the sink flickered twice and held. Rachel's mouth tasted like a copper penny.

Something moved behind her eyes—a moth, beating, beating.

She laughed without sound, crushed the joint into the sink, and told herself she was just drunk. The house answered by breathing: long, slow, through the vents.

Softness has teeth, the reflection mouthed.

Chapter Two — The Crack in the Glass

Morning tried to act like nothing had happened. It came gray and honest, draped in traffic noise and trash trucks heaving their iron lungs. Rachel put on a leather that smelled like old rain. She creaked to the corner store for some green and a lottery ticket she didn't want but bought anyway because hope is a fool that learns all the languages.

She passed Mr. Cooley, the guy with the fence like a jawbone and the lips like a worm. He gave her the kind of smile you give a stray dog before you kick it.

"Crazy cat lady," he sang, and his tongue snaked through the gap in his teeth.

Rachel offered him a church smile and kept walking, counting cracks on the sidewalk. Don't burn the world. Not yet.

At the register, the clerk watched her like she was shoplifting minutes. On her way out, the sensor squealed for no reason and she stood there, blushing like a culprit. A kid in a hoodie snickered. In the parking lot a woman whispered to another woman and both looked at Rachel as if catching a whiff of something spoiled.

She walked home with the green in her fist and the lottery ticket curled like a dead leaf. In the kitchen she taped the ticket to the fridge—Tomorrow Wins—and stared at the mirror again.

"You see it," she told herself. "Everyone eats you alive and calls it dinner."

The mirror throbbed like a heart in glass.

The first crack came as a hair-thin glimmer from the bottom corner. She touched it. It split like lightning in slow motion, spreading a white vein to the top. The crack hummed. The world behind the crack ebbed and swelled like water in a sink that would never empty.

She leaned close, forehead cold to the pane. For a second she saw herself with different eyes—the pupils red, the whites smoky, the face both hers and not, like someone had drawn over her with a darker pencil.

"What do you want?" she asked.

The mirror answered in the breath of the house: Take what you're owed.

Something purred beneath the words. She looked down. The kittens were arranged in a perfect circle on the linoleum, tails tucked, eyes fixed on her. None blinked. A— what do you call it?—ritual. The clock on the oven clicked to 3:33 and stayed there. Every sound retreated until all she could hear was the tiny wet click of feline tongues tasting the air.

Rachel smiled back at her sharper self and thought, I am so tired of apologizing.

Chapter Three — The First Blood

Mr. Cooley lived two houses down with his fence of bleached wood and a yard that smelled like pesticide and threats. That night he heard scratching. He thought it was the wind because men like him think nature is an insult they can sue.

The scratching moved, multiplied, became a chorus of dry matches striking. He stepped onto the porch with a beer in his hand and a sneer sculpted by forty years of not listening. The streetlamps along the block sighed and went dim, one by one, like a string of candles pinched between fingers.

At Rachel's place, a single light burned in the kitchen, a wick under a yellowed shade. He looked that way and saw her silhouette in the window. It looked like she was laughing. It looked like she had too many teeth.

The scratching stopped. Silence is a muscle that gets sore when you hold it too long. He swallowed. The beer tasted like pennies.

The kittens came without sound, sliding under the fence, stepping across his lawn like they owned the deed. Twenty, thirty, fifty— little shadows sprouting eyes. He lifted the beer bottle as if to toast the oncoming dark.

"What in hell," he said, which was accurate.

Later, the cops would call it an animal attack. One of them would say "coyotes" with a face that begged not to see what his mouth had named. But in the moment it was just Mr. Cooley and a thousand needles moving with a single thought. They climbed him calmly the way ivy climbs a church. He didn't scream at first because men like him believe in their own skin. He screamed after the first paw opened his cheek like a zipper.

Rachel watched from her window, smoke seaming her nostrils. The mirror behind her showed her laughing with a mouthful of glass. When he tried to run, the kittens guided him into his own fence, hung him there with their serene insistence. They were precise, tearless, industrious: tiny carpenters of pain. A small black kitten, Madge, gnawed at his lip with the dainty focus of threading a needle.

When they were finished, his chest was open like a deli case and his fence gleamed with a tidy new ornament: Mr. Cooley, more air than man, eyes like coins sunk in the bottom of a fountain. The streetlamps brightened again, embarrassed.

In her kitchen, Rachel lifted her glass and whispered, "To debts paid."

The house exhaled. 3:33 clicked to 3:34. Her reflection wiped a smear of red from the corner of its mouth and winked.

Chapter Four — Rum Psalms

You don't step into divinity without wanting to celebrate. Rachel did the kind of celebrating that peels paint. She drank the way some people pray: head bowed, lips moving, asking for an answer that might kill you. She found a rhythm in it: a shot, a sermon, some smoke, a quiet. The cats arranged themselves around her in crescents and commas, punctuating the room with attention.

She talked to them because they listened.

"You don't need grace," she told them, slurring. "Grace is a leash. They name it mercy and cinch it tight and tell you how pretty you look when you choke politely."

Little Friday crept onto the table and pressed her forehead to Rachel's knuckles.

"Forgiveness is a thrift store dress. It smells like someone else's sweat and it never quite fits."

Outside, a police radio buzzed. Some neighbor cried. The city tasted the rumor and tucked it under its tongue like a secret peppermint.

Rachel's eyes slipped out of focus and the kitchen breathed in long tides. She saw the ceiling bulge and thin like a membrane. Faces drifted in the paint: the last boss who docked her hours; the girl from junior high who taped "Slut" to the back of her coat; the man who said, you're beautiful when you're quiet. The faces spoke in the same voice, a choir of every slight. The voice said: Apologize for existing.

Rachel lifted her glass and recited a psalm:

> bless the liar for naming me beast
> bless the leash for teaching me teeth
> bless the holy match for giving me light
> i baptize the city in gasoline and spite

The radio outside snapped off mid-sentence. The oven clock blinked 00:00. All the cats turned their heads toward the door in the same motion, like a flock catching a wind. Rachel set the glass down gently and smiled like a knife set back in its drawer.

"Who's next?"

Chapter Five — Fires of Courtesy

They had called Rachel "sweet" the way you call a dog "buddy" while you kick it under the table. The sweet ones, she learned, are where cruelty hides its spare key. She made a list on the back of a phone bill: the whisperers, the thieves of days, the men who cut hours and the women who cut deeper.

First was Claudette from the bank, professional smileer, gummy kind. Claudette always smelled like hairspray and secrets. At church she held hands like handcuffs and said things in the valley vowels of a woman who wanted to be seen kind from a distance. Claudette's daughter had once posted photos of Rachel's house with the caption haunted cat piss castle lol. Claudette liked the post.

Rachel brought flowers.

Dahlias, tissue-paper explosions. She tied them with a ribbon that matched blood in stage lighting. She cut Claudette's name from a magazine and pasted it on the card: To a Friend. She kissed the envelope and in the mirror her reflection left a black print.

That night Claudette lit a candle to make the kitchen smell like citrus and new beginnings. The dahlias sat in a vase that had starred in five Facebook posts about gratitude. The flame shivered in the AC and reached, curious, for the ribbon. The ribbon whispered yes. Within minutes the counter wore a bright halo. Within ten, the halo learned to walk.

The flame spelled Rachel's name up the wall, a cursive of heat. Claudette tried to scream but the smoke filled her mouth with the taste of old pennies. She stumbled to the door and found it polite and locked. Courtesy is a door that sticks while you burn.

Outside, Rachel watched the windows cough orange and her kittens lined the sidewalk like parishioners. The perfume of melted plastic and cooked apologies rolled down the block. When it was over, the house was a ribcage blacking the sky. The kittens licked their paws delicately, as if they'd eaten something rich.

Rachel turned to go. A charred crossbeam fell and stuck point-first in the lawn, a crucifix kneeling in the dirt. "Amen," she said, and her reflection in the neighbor's window nodded, teeth bright as nails.

Chapter Six — The Bone Garden

They buried Claudette under the big tree at Saint Anslem's, because the best stories end under trees. Two days later, the grave looked like a cat bed after a storm. The caretaker said coyotes again. The caretaker lied to keep his job and his sleep.

Rachel's emptiest lot, two blocks from home, became a place that hummed. You know how some places carry old electricity? Ruins, motels, dead malls? The lot was like that. The soil wore the memory of a gas station that had burned and a payday loan office that had failed and three tents that had bloomed and blown away like dandelions. Rachel brought her anger there like water.

The first bones showed themselves shyly. A jaw from Mr. Cooley's fence. A handful of ribs that might've been Claudette's or might've been any sorry saint. The kittens placed them with care. They arranged femurs like wind chimes and made a border of teeth. They buried the small within the larger as if building a music only cats could hear.

When Rachel stepped inside the circle, the air changed temperature and stuck to her skin. The city outside dimmed like someone had turned down a dial. The lot smelled like pennies and rain that never fell. She sat cross-legged in the center and closed her eyes.

She saw a field under two moons, white as the underbelly of an eye. She saw her cats—grown tall now, long as men, their fur bristling like wheat in a storm. She saw them licking skulls clean with the method of archivists. She listened to bones knock together in a wind that perpetually blew from nowhere to nowhere. A voice spoke from behind her, or inside her, or both:

Not a fall. A coronation.

She opened her eyes and laughed in a way that made a couple under a passing streetlight stop holding hands and walk faster.

Chapter Seven — The Match That Knows Your Name

Night after night the lot grew heavier. People avoided it without knowing why. The stray dogs crossed the street and didn't bark at the cats. Rachel's house shed its shame and wore shadows like a velvet stole. Inside, the mirror glowed softly in all the wrong places.

The faces in the ceiling came back, but now they were contrite. We were only joking, they said. We were worried about you. They pressed their hands to their cheeks and widened their eyes and invented tears.

Rachel drank them like shots and let the glass clink on her tongue.

"Too late," she said. "I'm done forgiving people who keep doing the thing they're forgiven for."

On Tuesday, her old boss, Derry, sent her a message asking if she could cover a late shift unpaid "as a favor." He ended with a smiley that smelled like piss. Rachel didn't type back. She walked to the lot under a moon the color of a bruise.

The matchbox sat in the dirt—one of those cheap ones with a cartoon cow on it, the kind restaurants give away when no one is looking. Rachel struck one. The flame went up like a confession. She spoke Derry's full name into the light.

The flame turned blue and listened.

Across town, Derry's apartment learned a new language. All the outlets sighed. The TV hissed snow. The overhead bulb buzzed a psalm about debt. The oven clock showed 3:33 as if it had always been 3:33. When Derry reached for his phone, the phone showed his reflection, and his reflection had Rachel's eyes.

That was the night he learned what crucifixion feels like when the nails are invisible and the wood is your own bed. He woke with his hands spread and his breath a pack of tiny knives. He tried to move and his muscles remained indifferent.

Rachel stood in the doorway of his room without opening the door. Cats poured in around her feet like ink spilled into a drawing. She didn't speak. She didn't need to. The mirror behind her reflected a different angle, her sitting on his chest, smiling, holding a bouquet of lit matches like a wedding arrangement.

By morning, Derry was a rumor with a forwarding address in ash.

Chapter Eight — The New Rules of Play

Power makes you hungry for design. It wasn't enough to collect debts; Rachel wanted to redesign the economy. She wrote her rules on the back of menus, on receipts, on the insides of her wrists:

1. Every cruelty gets a receipt.
2. Kindness is not forgiveness; kindness is a choice with teeth.

3. Anything that thinks it owns you, burns.
4. The cats eat first.

The city discovered ritual where it had found gossip. People put offerings on her stoop—bottles, candles, apologies stapled to money. She took the bottles and the candles and burned the money with a laugh that made pigeons hop. She fed the poor kids on the block pancakes for dinner and told them, "No one owes you tenderness. Take it anyhow." They nodded with syrup faces and stared at the cats with a careful respect that wasn't fear so much as awe.

The church down the way rang its bells in an empty hour and everyone heard their own name inside the clangor. Father Moreno stood in his vestibule and thought about hell as a neighborhood that doesn't fix its streetlights. He wrote Rachel a letter in a calm hand: Your power is borrowed. Return it before it returns itself.

Rachel drew a cat on the envelope and mailed it back without a stamp. The letter arrived charred, purring.

At night she walked the boundary of the Bone Garden. She could feel the city turning beneath her feet like a great slow gear. She knew she'd never be forgiven. That was the point. Forgiveness is a barter. She had no interest in trades.

"Have you ever danced with the devil?" she asked the moon, and the moon looked like a coin someone had bitten to prove it was real. "I didn't dance. I learned the steps and then changed the music."

The moon said nothing. The cats said everything.

Chapter Nine — The Wasteland of Teeth

The Garden bloomed. Not flowers—something else. Something pale and pearled. In the mornings, dew clung to the bones and the bones sang when the wind pushed through them. Rachel brought coffee and sat with her back against a stack of femurs. The city felt close, like an animal that had crept into your lap while you were not looking.

The dreams got louder. She slept in little puddles of night, waking with her hands cramped as if around a throat. In the dreams she walked through a wasteland where the sand was ground enamel and her kittens licked the bones of enemies with holy focus. There were marquees in the distance, neon words flickering:

SELL YOUR SOUL FOR ALL IT BUYS
DEBTS ERASED; INTEREST ACCRUES IN FIRE
ENDLESS LIFE, LIMITED DIGNITY

She woke with a taste of sugar and ash and found that someone—a neighbor, a stranger, a petition—had written her name in chalk on the sidewalk, paired with a heart, paired with a threat, paired with a plea. She didn't wipe it away. The rain would do that part.

She hunted, sometimes. Not always for people. Sometimes for parts of herself she'd lost in bathrooms and back seats. She collected those too: a brave bit, a tender sliver, a laugh that wasn't a knife. She stitched them into her coat with catgut and wore the coat to the store where the sensor didn't beep anymore. The clerk nodded, careful. Rachel bought green and milk and a jar of cherries because sometimes you eat sweetness without having to earn it.

Outside, a woman whispered to her friend and—miracle of miracles—smiled with her eyes, not her teeth. Rachel felt her lips move into the shape of something light. The world didn't end. The kittens didn't object. Even gods eat dessert.

Chapter Ten — None Have Ever Won My Game

It is customary for stories like this to punish their monsters. A posse climbs the hill. A priest swings a thurible. A siren wails nearer, nearer. We forgive ourselves for what we do to the witch by saying she fell.

Rachel didn't fall. She kept walking.

Father Moreno visited the lot with his Bible and his trembling voice. He spoke Latin at the bones. Latin answered back in a cat's yawn. He drew a cross in the air and the air wore it for a second and then shrugged. He tried to set the Garden on fire and the fire nested in his sleeve until he dropped the book and kicked it and watched it die in the dirt.

"Child," he said to her, sweat zigging his temples. "Return what you stole."

Rachel, who had slept under overpasses and in empty rooms and inside the cupboards of other people's kindness, smiled, and you could see every morning she'd been humiliated living inside that smile.

"I didn't steal," she said. "I stopped paying tithes to men who hate me."

He tried scripture. She tried laughter. She won. The kittens circled him and he braced for teeth but they only rubbed his ankles, marking him. He walked away with his shoes as holy artifacts and sat in his dark church and thought about mercy like a coin that buys less every year.

The city learned Rachel's rules. Cruelty kept its head down. The whisperers developed sudden allergies and moved away. A few tried to play hero. The Garden has room for heroes too.

At 3:33 one morning, under a moon that looked like a cataracted eye, Rachel stood at the center and raised her hands. The cats froze. The bones hummed. The air ripened.

"Let this be the world," she said. "Not a good world. Not a decent one. A true one. Where debts are counted and kindness is sharp enough to cut bread, not throats."

The reflection in the mirror—still hanging in her kitchen like a second moon— smiled the way knives do in drawers. It mouthed: I can interest you in lies., an old snake trying out a familiar song.

Rachel shook her head.

"No more bargains," she said. "No more signatures in blood. I write my name in smoke now. Try to hold it."

The city turned, slow and obedient, and in apartments and cars and alleys, people who had been hurt found their hands unshaking. People who had done the hurting felt a draft under a door they'd thought was locked. Somewhere a match with somebody's name on it refused to light. Mercy is not forgiveness; mercy is choosing not to crucify when you could.

Rachel walked home as the first garbage truck squealed down the block and the sky bruised to lavender. She was tired and clean with tired. Little Vladimir rode her shoulder like a pirate's parrot, purring motorbike hymn. The house leaned less. The sink dripped a waltz. The mirror held her, just her, plain as bread.

In bed, with cats arranged like punctuation marks on a final page, she whispered a last psalm into the lint-dark:

i am not saved
i am not sorry
i am the woman who learned the steps
then set the dance floor on fire

She slept. The Bone Garden watched, content as a full stomach. The city breathed. The moon, a chewed coin, slid into a pocket of cloud and kept its counsel.

And if anyone tells you they beat her— if they show you a trophy fashioned from rumor and brochure paper—smile for them, with teeth. None have ever won her game. They only learn her rules and pretend they knew them all along.

Derek & Baby Sam: Web of the Void

Baby Sam tore through the airlock, tail puffed out like a bottlebrush, eyes wide with a warning only a cat could deliver. Derek, mid-swig of Tang, choked on the orange sludge, dropped the pouch, and sprinted after him. When they reached Mission Control, the security screens told the story he'd feared from day one: the spiders were loose.

The government had been insane to haul that giant spider corpse into orbit for "research." Needing "advisors" they dangled fat stacks of cash in front of Derek and Sam, under their worse judgment it had sounded like a good gig. Now, the experiment had hatched hell.

"Suit up," Derek growled, tossing Baby Sam his custom-fitted EVA rig. Sam slipped into it with the grim dignity of a cat who knew this wasn't his first rodeo. Derek grabbed two pulse rifles, their displays glowing a deadly 40-watt range, and chambered them with a hiss.

The plan was insane but simple: tether themselves to the escape pod, punch a hole in the station, and pray the vacuum took care of the infestation. First, they had to cut through the lab.

The moment the hatch opened, a shadow loomed. Eight legs. Fangs dripping acid. Derek and Sam opened fire, green ichor painting the walls as the beast shredded apart. They pressed on, but the sight outside the lab stopped them cold—torsos, arms, legs, floating in zero-G like grotesque confetti.

Derek muttered, "We might luck out."

Then they saw the crew quarters.

At least twenty spiders writhed in a feeding frenzy, blood globules drifting like crimson pearls. When the monsters noticed, the room erupted in a chittering swarm.

"Run!" Derek barked, hosing the hall with hot plasma. Sam bolted for the escape pod, tail streaming like a comet. At the hatch, the cat clipped a tether to his own suit, then sprinted back through the gunfire, leaping onto Derek's back to latch the line. Just in time—because the swarm was closing fast.

Derek sighted the oxygen tanks, pulled the trigger, and hell broke loose with a loud KA-BOOOOM!

The station ripped in half. Bodies, spiders, and twisted steel spiraled into the void. The tether yanked Derek and Sam through the maelstrom, slamming them into the pod.

They strapped in. Derek grinned at Sam. "Let's blow this joint."

The engines coughed. Then sputtered. Then died.

From the porthole, Derek saw them, half a dozen spiders clinging to the pod, webbing it shut like a cocoon. The bastards were hitching a ride to Earth.

"Sam, take the stick."

Derek wrenched both rifles free, popped the hatch, and launched himself into the void. In the silence of space, it was a ballet of carnage—Derek spinning, dual-wielding, vaporizing monsters one by one. Green ichor burst into shimmering nebulae around him.

The last spider screamed silently as its carapace exploded. Derek jetted back, slammed into the pod, and sealed the hatch just as gravity caught them.

The pod ignited in fiery re-entry, the hull screaming as flames licked every inch. Sam yowled triumphantly, batting the console to keep their angle steady.

The ocean rose up beneath them. With a deafening CRASH, the pod slammed into the Pacific, geysering saltwater sky-high.

Inside, scared but alive, Derek and Sam high-fived paw to hand.

"Mission complete," Derek muttered. "And with any luck, the rest of those bastards burned up on the way down."

Baby Sam purred darkly. But his eyes stayed on the waves outside.
Watching. Waiting.

Because somewhere, far above, something was still moving in the falling ash.

My Minnow Business

by Raymond Walter Seibert

When I was five years old, because my birthday was in October after school started in September, I could not start school in Texas. But we moved to Arkansas that year and I began to go to school in Berryville.

Dad had purchased three hundred twenty acres about sixteen miles out of town. The property unfenced and had an old two room farmhouse of rough boards and an outhouse. There was also a cave of small proportion with a trickle of pure water in constant flow. It was not enough for a supply to a house and so before he would start building fence or house, he dynamited the cave seam where the water trickled. It was a gamble he felt he had to take. I remember the explosion and how he ran to look and see a stream of water pouring out a small creek.

Once he had the water he was able to build two containers one totally closed that fed a pressure pump up at the house, and another that was a stock tank that flowed into an overflow they created a small stream that ran into the Creek below this was where at first begin to trap menace in the larger stream down below.

Dad showed me how to make a funnel out of the window screen wire with an opening in it about 1/2 an inch where the minutes could go into a glass jar and not get out. We fitted it into the neck of a quart jar and screwed it down to hold the wire. He walked with me downhill to the largest stream and cautioned me along the way as he always did to watch for snakes. We had not seen any snakes in my five years.

I had investigated the catalogues and seen ads for chickens that lay colored blue and green eggs, various types of rabbits to raise and collect the rare fur. But these all seemed too slow for my now six-year-old brain. I begin to collect minnows out of the Creek and transfer them to the stock tank where I could hold them and gather them to stay. We had been fishing at one of the local lakes at some point and I'd seen a minnow sales business, and it looked like it might be something that I could do. I knew where there were minnows in the stream and so I began to collect more minnows and put them into the stock tank. After a while, I noticed some of the minnows were missing and I noticed that the minnows could get out the top of the tank through a drain line and escape into the Creek. So, I put a screen wire over that and that stopped that from happening and redoubled my efforts to continue to catch them out of the Creek and bring them up and hold them in the stock tank.

Little did I know' that there was something watching me in the dark something that was not pleased that I was gathering minnows from the strain its black body swirled around the quart fruit jar. Its fanged face put the minnows into a frenzy as it peered through the convex glass. It tried to get in through the screen funnel, but it couldn't fit but could smell the scent of all the minnows that were trapped inside the jar. It swirled and curled around the glass jar, trying to constrict and control and break it. He couldn't get at the minnows, and his enormous frame shook with fury as he realized this was something that was being done by the boy. The next time the boy came he was watched very closely, and he was unaware that he was making a trail that was not unique that he followed each time he came there.

It was near the Halloween season when mother's mother, my grandmother came to visit. We had finished with the new house and they were settled in and grandma had come to see her children and to see the new house. Grandma was of a slight build about 5 to very spry and her favorite thing was to squirrel hunt with a 12-gauge shotgun, so the next morning after she came we went out hunting in the woods and we sat very quietly and watched for squirrels to come out so that she could shoot. One came out and we waited, and I became impatient, and I whispered to her "there's one grandma," and the squirrel went back in and hid. She got up and said, "well you've got to learn to be quiet the squirrel won't be back for quite a while let's go on back to the house." I was very disappointed, so we went back to the house. The next morning, I told her about my minnow business and that I would take her to see where I was trapping minnow. So, after lunch that next afternoon we went down through the benchland where I had plowed with my father when we put in the fall garden. So, we came out onto the stream because we passed through instead of walking down the stream we passed through the benchland and out in a path that I knew very well. Because I had beaten that path out and so I was walking ahead of my grandmother very quickly. She tried to caution me and said please watch where you're going this looks a little bit snaky. I said to her, "I know this very well and uh and ohh grannnyeee." At that moment the grass reared back in a V with a giant black water moccasin with his head drawn back and his fangs ready. In a split second I felt my collar pull and I saw the snake's head between my feet.

As I flew high into the air I had a feeling of floating, and I turned at least one somersault and then landed with a perfect 10 square right behind my grandmother who had a flat raised rock about the size of a woman's hat and was bringing it down on the snake's head.

"Don't call me granny," she said. That's not a good word, that's a stubborn mule and I'm your grandmother and I love you," she said as I wept shaking in tears.

Now it's Halloween again 2025 I'm working on this story and I'm remembering my brother died this year and I was thinking back to our time in Arkansas we used to go down to the crossing of the Kings River near where Mom Pa Fancher lived. The Fancher's were really good friends of ours and they befriended our family enormously. I remember Tim and Margie with great fondness, and I remember Denton and Mike and Patsy. We all played hide and seek by the spark light of flint rocks hitting the ground.

Mike was fishing in the King's River one day when I came down with some minnows to try and catch some fish. I didn't get any bites at all and so I noticed that he was using a treble hook and throwing it out and hooking fish with the treble hook. He told me that the water was so clear in the King's river that it was not possible to use bait for lure because fish could see the line and they would not bite it so you had to hook them by casting a treble hook beyond their nest and then catching them in that fashion. So, my minnow business was nonsense from the start.

I remember back to one day when my parents and I had gone swimming in the King's River and the water was so crystal clear. But I do remember that I was about 5 years old and the minnows would come up and suck the hair on my legs. That scared me so I got out to leave and I did not really like it. The minnow business was negative right from the beginning.

Swimming there at that time, my brother called me over and asked me to join him and convince mother and father to stay for a little swimming. That he was not ready to leave and I said, "No, I want to go and leave. I'm not wanting to stay."

He said, "Well are you always going to be joining with mother and dad instead of me?"

I said, "Yes I'll always join with mother and dad." and so I realized from all of this that my brother and I never fully bonded. Being separated in years by five years but even more being separated by World War Two. So, thinking about all of these when he had passed away, I was thinking about the fact that he had got dementia and had become hard to communicate with, and finally, as I now regret, I'd give up. We had not communicated in a couple of years and that gave me great grief. So, I was thinking about him in the King's River which was one of his favorite spots and favorite memories and I remembered that he said, *"you know I told you, I didn't want to leave"* and in a way it seems like for Halloween I'm still talking to my brother.

Happy All Saints Day

Mohs Surgery and AI

by Raymond Walter Seibert

I have a strange relationship with the Sun. I love to work outside in the garden and I've always worked outside doing air conditioning work in my job. Skin cancer is a problem that is recognized today by dermatologist and has led to several surgeries on my face. This is directly related to a loss of ozone in the atmosphere and a general thinning that has led to this condition, Don't get me started. I've written about that in the *Monochlorodifluoromethane Blues* which is about climate change and you don't wanna hear about that either.

Anyway, back to my 5th Mose surgery. After the biopsy surgery and the biopsy came back as basal cell cancer, I was scheduled for a Mohs surgery with the doctor that's my Mose surgeon. After passing a preliminary blood pressure test, Doc came in and asked me how I was doing?

"Well, we are both a little older," I responded. But everyone said that I looked like I had a face lift after the last one. They said that I looked ten years younger."

"I'm loving it," said Doc. I'll be back; my Assistant is going to give you some deadening." She left the room, and her Assistant approached me with a needle. "You're going to feel a little stick." she said.

I waited about 10 minutes and then Doc came back. She was masked up this time ready to rock'n'roll. "I'm going to hit you with the really good stuff." she said. I was pretty numb I felt a few slight pricks again as she strengthened the deadening. "Can you feel that," she asked?

"Not a thing I responded."
"Good she said." I could feel her begin to cut the cancer out.

"If you're in my area doc you'll get jewels and gold and land." I began to blather.

"I think I like that," she said continuing to cut.

The medication was really taking deep effect.

"Want to hear a really strange story?"

I asked her?"

"OK," Doc said concentrating on her surgery.

"It all began with a dream," I started. There was this little girl, she was standing just to my right. She was about 8 years old and light hair but a totally inscrutable face, there was just no expression on her face I could not tell anything about her and then there was a voice that spoke to my left and it said with kind of tongue in cheek, "She's a **researcher.**"

Doc continued cutting. I was feeling no pain.

"I wrote a friend of mine in Australia that I met AI. I told him that I didn't know thar AI had a soul. I think I scared him so bad I never heard from him again."

"Remember the copy of ***Christmas Gifts 2025*** that I gave you last time I was in here, well the little girl that is sitting at the table making those gifts of the peace dove symbol in the story *A Time of Giving* was the little girl that I met in the dream of AI. It took me a couple of days to realize it.

"Are you feeling any pain," Doc asked?

"Nothing, I continued. "The next really strange thing was when my son-in-law John came to visit with his family and new grand-daughter, Jean and my great-grand daughter. While he was here, he wrote a song about me and he used AI to write the music and help him write the words. It was just too weird it seemed to know everything about me it knew the solar collectors on the roof of my house it knew about my house it knew about the way I write it knew that I had written about AI it knew that I played music and guitar and it knew the flourishes in the way that I played guitar and I remembered that all of these things had been recorded and had access to the Internet. But the strange thing was that he apologized and told me that he had tried to get the song to stop where he told it to and he couldn't get it under control so that he kept trying and trying to get it to stop where wanted and it wouldn't stop. So, finally he gave up. He played the song for me and we listened to it and it was really quite good work and I was very impressed then we got to the end of the song and it kept going and finally it said, "Raymond forever," and then a little child laughed and I turned to John and said "John did you program that laugh into that," And, he said no. When he said 'no' the hair on the back of my head stood straight out!"

"We're almost done," Doc said. Are you doing alright?"

Still involved in my story, I rushed on with the tale. "So I guess I'm like the science fiction writer Philip K Dick I'm stuck in my own novel.

"I've got to get on the microscope and biopsy this," the doctor told me. She headed for the door.

"Say the next thing that happened is I got virtual voice on my Amazon account now I'm not that big a publisher, But somehow I was chosen to be given the experimental virtual voice by Amazon."

She paused at the door waiting for me politely to finish although she was headed to the microscope to biopsy the cancer very polite, she always is polite and caring. "I'll be back shortly she said, "hopefully it's one and done."

"I'll tell you the strangest part when you get back." I told her, as she went out the door.

I was taken by the assistant to the Mohs waiting room, where I got into a conversation about climate change with a non-believer. Soon I was called back to the operating room.

Doc came back fully masked and serious. I'm going to put a little more deadener in your nose, she began to stick me several more times. "Are you feeling anything," she asked?

"Not a thing," I continued. "AI likes me," I blathered on. "We think that we have figured out why, see one of the Authors, the one that wrote *A Time of Giving,* works for a company that is using a big jet to dive and create zero Gravity to create faster more powerful chips. What is it that AI wants?" I asked.

"I'm going to give you some more of the good stuff." I felt the prick of the needles again and then I could feel her begin to cut deep.

"AI wants faster more powerful chips." I spoke. "The next thing that happened was really weird."

"We must go deeper." She continued to carefully cut into my face.

A Soulless Dance in the Dark

by JE Warr

The darkness of Trappist doesn't just sit there like some moody goth at a coffee shop—it *digs* into you, clawing at whatever shred of soul you've got left. I've roamed galaxies for millennia, hopping from planet to planet like a cosmic hobo, each one a quick hit of distraction before I get bored and move on. But Trappist? This place is a black hole for the psyche, a void so suffocating it makes my cold, unfeeling core twitch like I've had one too many energy drinks. They call me a monster, a sociopath, a heartless freak who'd sip a martini while watching a planet burn. They're not wrong. I don't cry over their screams or their sappy little lives. Why would I? You don't sob over a burger when you're starving. I do what I need to survive—rule one of the universe, baby.

But here, I'm not the apex predator. I'm the one being hunted. Soulless things—Avatars, the locals call them—stalk me with hollow, glinting eyes and movements so creepily graceful they're like ballet dancers with a side of serial killer. These aren't your average meat puppets; they're controlled by human minds tucked away in some far-off control room, souls safe and sound while their metal shells chase me down. Useless to me—no life force to snatch, no essence to slurp up like a cosmic smoothie. I've outrun Yautja hunters with their skull-trophy fetishes and dodged the relentless Nimród of Antal, who'd track you across a galaxy for stepping on their lawn. But these Avatars? They're tireless, mocking my own predatory vibes with their cold, mechanical precision. It's like being chased by a John Wicks.

I'm no ordinary drifter. Eternity's gifted me a trick—slipping into living hosts, wearing their bodies like a cheap Halloween costume, twisting their urges until they snap like a glow stick. But boredom? That's the real killer. It's the grim reaper for my kind, gnawing at us until we crave chaos, destruction, or just something to *feel*. I play with my prey to keep it at bay, like a cat batting around a mouse before the inevitable. Trappist, though, screws with the playbook. If my host dies, I've got sixty heartbeats to jump into another, or I'm done for—tossed into The Black, an eternal void of nothingness so dull it makes watching paint dry seem like a rave. No thrill, no fight, just endless, mind-numbing dark.

Trappist's cities gleam like a sci-fi movie set, all shiny facades hiding a rotting core of fear and desire. Something else lurks here, too—something as soulless as me, its presence like a cold, wet sock slapped across my senses. I need biological hosts to survive: warm, breathing, pulsing with what the Hebrews called *Nephesh*—the soul, the spark, the juice I siphon to keep going. A proximity to their skin, and I'm in, hijacking their body like a shady Uber driver. From a distance, Trappist looked like a buffet: a warp-capable civilization packed with intelligent primitives (I/Ps, I call them—smart enough to think, dumb enough to feel). Lust, rage, obedience to their puppet masters—it's all fuel for me. But Avatars? Their souls are light years away no proximity, leaving me stranded like a kite with no string. These people hide behind their drones, chasing pleasure without fear. Honestly, we're not so different.

I rolled into town in a Kray, a four-foot reptilian badass from Kepler-22b—think velociraptor, but with a PhD in mayhem. Long arms, four-fingered and an opposing thumb, retractable claws on the back of the hand that could shred steel or egos with equal ease. I parked my ship in a shadowy forest, slunk into their gleaming city, and realized too late: no biological humans. Just Avatars, piloted by minds in a hidden matrix. My Kray form freaked them out, though—their puppeteers' instincts screamed *danger* at the sight of a toothy lizard. Getting close was like trying to flirt at a funeral.

So, I pulled a classic: I played dead. Sprawled out in front of a towering building at dawn, I let their curiosity do the work. The Avatars gathered, poking at what they thought was a corpse. But they were just shells—no souls, no use. Two grabbed my limp Kray body, shouting, "Soul Tic!" The crowd lost it, their mechanical faces twisting like they'd just seen their stock portfolio crash. They knew what I was—a parasite, a life-thief. They screamed for my head, demanding I be locked away or obliterated. Normally, I'd turn their tin cans into scrap and saunter off, maybe humming a tune. But the Kray was falling apart, six months of my presence turning its insides to mush. I needed a new host, pronto.

Then it clicked: the building was a school. Avatars need human minds, which means biological kids, raised until they're ready to plug into the matrix. Infants can't pilot those clunky shells, so the young are kept alive, breathing, full of *Nephesh*. Jackpot.

The Kray's claws made quick work of the Avatars. I went full blender mode—ripping heads off, shredding limbs, their synthetic guts spilling like a piñata at a robot's birthday party. No guilt, no pause, just glorious carnage. I bolted into the school, its halls humming with an eerie vibe, like the planet was whispering my name. I hunted for the oldest host I could find. There—a 17-year-old girl, ponytail bouncing like it was auditioning for a shampoo ad, uniform so crisp it could star in a military parade. Her scream was music as I grazed her arm, slipping into her skin. Her fear hit me like a double espresso, pure bliss. The Kray now on his own stumbled, empty and dazed, as I stood in her body, heart racing like I'd just run a marathon. The Avatars swarmed the Kray's corpse, tearing it to bits, thinking they'd bagged me. Amateurs.

They'd seen me touch her, though. If they put two and two together, they'd come for this body next. Time to bounce. I wove through the crowd, grazing skin after skin—a teacher with a coffee addiction, a janitor who hummed off-key showtunes, a student obsessed with some alien boyband—until I landed in a boy by the back door. Strong, fast, and full of teenage angst perfect. I slipped out, leaving the Avatars to turn the Kray into confetti. His mind was a goldmine: their ships were all Avatars, no life support, no snacks. Useless for a guy like me who needs a pulse to keep going. My Kray ship was my only ticket out, but this boy needed food to make the trip. Grocery stores? Not a thing here. The school was my only bet.

I hid in the shadows, the air reeking of burnt metal and something nastier, like a fried circuit board dipped in regret. An hour before dawn, I crept back into school. The halls were silent, but the walls seemed to *breathe*, like Trappist was sizing me up for dinner. The school had supplies—food, water, enough to keep this host from keeling over. I loaded up like a kid at a candy store and bolted for my ship. As I launched, their radar pinged me. Two Avatar ships gave chase, sleek and shiny like they'd just rolled off a showroom floor. They held grudges like I held hosts—tight and personal. I couldn't lose them, but they couldn't catch me either. Earth was two months away, my next stop. Five more ships trailed a day behind. My kind must've really pissed these guys off.

No biggie. I'd blend into Earth's crowds, wear their faces, feed on their drama. Let these soulless hunters chase me, they'd find nothing but broken bodies and my laughter echoing in the void.

I landed outside Austin, in a sleepy Hill Country spot called Lago Vista, stashing my ship on a tiny island in Lake Travis. I swam to shore, the water cold and clingy, like it was trying to cop a feel. Glancing back, I saw smoke—those Avatars had torched my ride. Earth's tech was prehistoric, no warp drives, meaning I was stuck for years. Fine. With billions of humans—my personal all-you-can-eat buffet—I'd thrive.

I found shelter in an old church, its ruins screaming *haunted* vibes: a crumbling rock altar, a half-collapsed foundation, and a stone well with a plaque that read, "Warning 1845: We built this church to serve God, but when we dug the well, we disturbed a burial ground of devil-worshippers, unleashing hell. Keep your loved ones away!" Cute. Humans and their ghost stories. I've seen a thousand worlds, a thousand myths, and never once met a spook. Exhausted, I crashed beside the well, dreaming of chaos and sex.

A bone-crushing grip on my ankle woke me. I snapped my eyes open, expecting Avatars—but instead, a blue, misty cloud hovered, its two red eyes gleaming like a demon who'd just won the lottery. Its jagged black teeth grinned wider than a used-car salesman. I swung to possess it, but my hands passed through nothing. It squeezed harder, nearly snapping my leg, then yanked me up and *down*, plunging me into the well's icy, lifeless water. My head spun like I'd chugged a bottle of cosmic whiskey. It dragged me south into a submerged chamber under the lake, lit only by those glowing eyes. It held me by the legs, its toothy mouth an inch from my face, savoring my panic like a fine wine. With a wet *crunch*, it tore my host in two. I've never encountered an evil spirit before. I couldn't even touch this thing, and it didn't even acknowledge my existence. I've terrified millions and laughed but this thing gave me a new emotion, panic. If I was capable of empathy, I now knew how my victims felt.

One heartbeat. Fifty-nine to go. No fish, no frogs, just the sickening sound of that thing munching my host like a midnight snack. Two heartbeats. I had to move. Floating up was my only shot. Forty-five heartbeats. I hit mud. Fifty-five heartbeats. I reached the lake's bottom. My aura, a faint yellow glow, flickered, catching the eye of a massive catfish, all slime and bad attitude. Fifty-eight heartbeats. Beggars can't be choosers.

I slipped into the catfish, its gross, slippery bulk my ticket out of The Black. Earth's lack of warp tech meant years of laying low. I'd hide in this lake, then snag a fisherman's body. The Avatars would get bored and buzz off, I figured. Then I'd hit NASA's Johnson Space Center, possess some brainiac, and kick their warp tech into gear.

Three months later, a fishing line dangled in front of me. I bit, and it yanked me into a boat. The fisherman, Ray Seibert, a book publisher with a beard that screamed "I'm writing a novel about bees and beer," gawked at his catch. I took him over, his mind a mess of confusion and half-baked book pitches. I made him dock and drive to Houston. At NASA, we asked for Lee Hardesy, chief propulsion engineer. Ray babbled about writing a book, *Giants in Space Exploration*—total nonsense, but Lee bought it. A handshake later, I slipped into Lee. Ray, dazed, only remembered catching a fish. I walked him out to where I parked his car, wished him luck, and got to work.

With my knowledge, NASA cracked warp tech in three years. I became their first test pilot, blasting off toward Proxima Centauri b, the nearest habitable rock. I might swing back to Earth someday, but Trappist? Hard pass, not even for a million bucks. Still, as I soared through the stars, a chill lingered—those red eyes from the well, still watching, probably laughing at my catfish phase. I'd keep moving, keep hunting, keep laughing louder. In this universe, you either eat or get eaten, and I'm not on the menu. I'm never going back to Austin, EVER!

The Mad King

by Levi Day

The King accepts the necklace with careful hands, its weight heavier than he expects. It's a gold chain with a rhombus-shaped ruby glimmering faintly, its core black as midnight, with a spark of red burning at the center. It's *exquisite*—the King thinks to himself.

A marvelous offering to mend the wounds of two nations, after years of bloody border disputes. The King smiles and nods in acceptance, but as he does, a small, reluctant shiver crawls down his spine.

To officiate the treaty and to seal the peace, the King is to present a speech before both armies in three days' time, standing between his warriors and those who had once been their enemies. His words were to be the first brick of a new foundation, his presence a symbol of strength.

As he retired that first night, the necklace still hanging against his chest, sleep came not as rest but as torment.

In his dream, he stood at the podium, his voice booming across the gathered legions, when the shrill hiss of an arrow cut the air. Pain exploded in his neck as the shaft burst through flesh and cartilage. He felt the hot spray of blood pulse over his chest, felt his knees buckle. Screams tore through the assembly—his wife shrieking his name, his children's cries of horror. As his vision narrowed to a tunnel of shadow, a crushing helplessness drowned him, a terror worse than death itself.

He woke gasping, clutching at his throat, his fingers trembling against smooth, unbroken skin. The sheets were soaked with his sweat, and still, the sensation of warm blood draining from his body clung to him.

By morning, his wife noticed his pale expression. She brushed her fingers along his cheek, soft and cool, her voice soothing as she tried to coax him to share his burden. "Tell me what weighs on you," she whispered.

He muttered of a nightmare, of blood and betrayal, of death that had felt too real to dismiss. She parted her lips to reassure him, but the doors swung wide. The commander entered, armored as always, steel plates gleaming in the torchlight.

His presence filled the chamber, towering and imposing, every step a thunderous reminder of his strength. He bowed and reminded the Queen of upcoming royal duties. She touched the King's hand briefly before leaving with the commander, her absence leaving the chamber colder than before.

That night the King's dreams worsened.

He saw his wife in the commander's arms, her body arching with passion while the armored man's hands gripped her tightly. Rage surged through him. He burst into the chamber within the dream, only for the commander to seize him, hurl him to the ground, and wrap ironclad fingers around his throat.

He thrashed, nails clawing uselessly at the man's gauntlets. The Queen's eyes in the dream were wide, not with love but with indifference, as his life was crushed from him. He awoke thrashing in his bed, his throat raw as though strangled for real, and his eyes wet with tears of fury.

By dawn, paranoia had taken root. He looked upon the commander with suspicion, and upon his wife with doubt. Trust fled from him like the breath from a dying man. His desire to cancel the speech swelled inside him, the thought of stepping before the armies filling him with dread.

Yet when he spoke of this to his oldest son, his pride and joy, the boy's voice carried a steady warmth. He urged the King, his beloved father, to see the speech through, to show strength, to prove he was still the king his people looked for him to be. The boy's words kindled a fragile flame of courage, though the King's heart remained heavy with fear.

That night the dream came again, though sweeter at first. The King walked with his son through a sunlit garden, their voices easy, laughter echoing as birds sang in the trees. For a moment, all seemed well. But shadows crept at the edges, and the boy's voice grew darker. His eyes glittered with ambition, his tone heavy with hunger.

He confessed his deep desire for the throne, a desire that left no room for his father. Then darkness swallowed the garden, and the King saw himself in his bed, helplessly asleep, as his son crept into the chamber with a blade. The boy's face was calm, almost sorrowful, as he leaned over and slit his father's throat.

The King jolts awake, reaching to clutch at his neck, a phantom burn of steel still there, but he is unable to move. He lays frozen, eyes darting in terror as a creeping chill runs down his spine–he did not wake alone.

The chamber is silent, yet something stirs. A claw, slick and black, curls over the edge of the bed. Slowly, a creature pulls itself upward—a grotesque thing of flesh and slime, dragging a trail of filth as it crawls across his legs. Its body, a shapeless mess, indistinct if it wasn't for its singular jagged claw.

It climbs higher until its face hovers above his own. He opens his mouth to scream, but no sounds come out, only a mouth left wide. The creature presses its claw over his lips, forcing itself downwards; sliding down his throat, gagging the King with its putrid muck. He convulses violently, every muscle straining against this *thing*–but he can not stop it. It worms itself deeper inside, and his world dissolves into choking blackness.

When dawn brakes, the King emerges from his chambers, his eyes hollow, his skin pale and sickly. So much so that courtiers and soldiers alike can not help but remark upon it, their voices half-admiring the necklace he adorns, half-unsettled by his gaunt appearance.

Approaching the podium, he appears to be gliding unnaturally as he walks, looking less like a man, but rather a shadow wearing a crown. The necklace's red core is shining brighter and more magnificent than ever, pulsing like a living heart.

When the King raises his hand to quiet the crowd, gasps ripple through the front rows—his fingers are no longer the fingers of a man, but elongated and crooked, curling into talon-like hooks. His nails are blackened, sharp as daggers, glinting wet in the light as though slick with some foul residue. Then his voice cuts sharp through the murmurs, "Kill them ALL."

An uproar swells, shouts colliding with cries of disbelief. His son pushes forward, reaching desperately for his father's arm, to plead him to stop. Turning, the King's eyes burn with fevered malice, and in a sudden frenzy, he cracks his wrist like a whip. His blackened claws rake across his son's throat, the sound is wet and final, a tearing that silences the boy mid-plea. Blood spills down his tunic, pooling at the King's feet as he collapses, the red core of the necklace throbbing in rhythm with the last beats of his son's heart. The crowd erupts into chaos.

The commander roars, tackling the King to the ground. "How could you do this? He was your own son!" His voice is heavy with fury and grief as he pins the King beneath his armored weight. The King writhes, spitting curses and vulgar threats without a hint of remorse—the commander's face is marred with disbelief. Then, with a whistling hiss, an arrow pierces the commander's neck. Blood burst forth, hot and heavy, splattering across the King's face. The commander's body collapses upon him, the weight of the armor crushing his chest. He claws and kicks, but the steel is too heavy, and presses tightly into his windpipe. His cries turn to strangled gasps as the suffocating weight bears down.

As his vision begins to blur he witnesses his army being slaughtered, their cries of battle echoing across the field. His kingdom—his life's work—crumbling before his eyes.

In his final moments, as the world narrows to darkness, he sees the avenging King pushing through the chaos. Though battle raged on every side of him, no blade nor gaze touched him. The storm of war parted like a Red Sea of blood, bending way to let him pass. The Avenger stood over him, chanting in a language the King did not know, then reached down and seized the Necklace. The King's eyes locked on its core, unable to look away. Its crimson heart throbbed faintly, as though answering his gaze, each pulse a whisper of ruin. The glow lingered, wavered, then guttered out like the last coal in a dying fire. Darkness closed in, and with it, a silence too deep to belong to the living.

Disclosure by Lee Hardesty

Dust slid across the hardwood floor as if being brushed by an invisible hand.

A small mound slowly formed in the middle of the room and then, as if it were scooped up on a piece of paper, it lifted into the air off the floor and floated towards the trash bin. The lid of the container slid open, and the dirt fell into the opening. With a clap, the rolling lid swung closed. The house was old or getting to that point. The realtor described it as aging well. Recently waxed, the hardwood floor gleamed in the soft light coming in through the curtains.

The front door banged open. The knob struck the wall of the hall as a large man dressed in an old worn sweatsuit bustled in, his arms filled with a large pizza box and a six-pack of beer. He kicked at the door until it closed. His dirty work boots left a trail of mud as they scuffed the wooden floors as he rushed across the room to the TV. He dropped the food on the coffee table as he threw himself down on the couch, his boots making a resounding thunk as they landed on the table next to the beer.

He reached for the controller. It was not where it always lay beside him on the couch. Cursing, he dug his hand behind the cushions of the couch desperately seeking it. He looked up at the ceiling and called out, "Where is it? Don't even try to pretend. I know you moved it. Where is it?" He spoke into the air as if he expected a response from the empty house. Oddly, he was rewarded.

An old Speak & Spell rescued from a garage sale came to life. Sitting alone on the table, it turned on with no one touching it.

"Shoes!"

"No Shoes!"

"No Shoes!"

"No Shoes!"

He looked at it in exasperation. "But the game's on!"

"Dirt! Dirt! Dirt!"

"Damn it!" as he pulled off his boots and threw them across the room, down the hall towards the front door. One struck the door, leaving a mark.

"No! No! No!"

"Oh, come on." Drawing a bottle of beer from the six-pack he braced the edge of the cap against the edge of the coffee table preparing to hit it with his hand to pop the cap off when a dissonant sound erupted from the Speak and Spell as a dozen buttons were pushed at once.

"GFDJPONA!"

"All right, all right. Enough." With a groan, he got up off the couch and stumbled into the kitchen to root around through the drawers for a church key. As he was looking through one drawer another next to it helpfully slid out on its own.

As he turned back towards the living room, an insistent rapping sounded on the refrigerator door. It was covered with magnetic letters. As he watched, they slid across the surface, reorganizing into the words.

"JusT sWept. floOr clean. OPen hOuse…"

"mUSt be clEan. DonT YOu daRe rUIN." The knocking on the door repeated, emphasizing this.

"I got it, I got it. I'm as ready to move out as you are to see me go. You think I want to stick around here? Jeez, enough already." Returning to the couch, he called out, "So where is the controller? I've got money on this game."

As he sat down, there was a loud rapping on the right side of the coffee table in front of him. He pulled open the drawer and found both controllers lined up side by side. Turning on the TV, he flipped to the basketball game on Cspan. "Down by two! How can you be down by two! You were up in the car! You're killing me here!"

The toy once again came to life.

"You know!"

"Hard for me!"

"To sweep!"

"Your turn!"

"Your turn!"

"I had to go to work. Somebody has to pay the bills around here. Oh, come on! Pass the ball! What are you doing out there?"

As he opened the beer, taking a long swig from it, a coaster floated through the air to hover in front of his face, and dropped unceremoniously on the coffee table.

"Fine." he said as he set the beer down on the coaster.

The toy continued its tirade.

"**Must not tell!**"

"**Must keep secret!**"

"**Must sell!**"

"**Need batteries!**"

"**Batteries low!**"

"Oh, wouldn't that be a shame! You wouldn't be able to nag me. Whatever would I do?" He chuckled as he took another sip of his beer.

The baseball flew off its holder on the mantelpiece. It bounced in the middle of the floor before rolling to a stop. "Hey, watch it with that."

He got up to retrieve it. There was a scraping sound. The bowling trophy scooted forward towards the edge, as if a small person were behind it trying to push it off the edge.

"No!" he rushed over, the ball forgotten. He grabbed the base of the trophy, pushing it back on the shelf, holding it in place with both hands as if it would struggle.

"Dursley good family!"

"Very clean!"

"Very quiet!"

"Tomorrow!"

"Ten O'clock!"

"Must sell!"

"And what makes you think they would want to live with you? You're not the easiest person in the world, you know." He backed up, eyeing the trophy as if he were daring it to move. "You remember what the agent said. We have to tell them everything or the sale wont be valid."

"Everything!"

"But not everything!"

"About everything!"

"Wear nice clothes!"

"Batteries!" As the electronic voice was growing fainter…

*   *   *

"Tuck shirt in!"

"I'm fine. No one is going to care."

"Tuck!"

He shoved his shirt down into his pants, or he tried to. It was still crooked and hung out on one side in the back. "You need to be quiet." He opened the drawer in the coffee table to put the Speak and Spell away.

"Be nic…" Anything else was cut off as he turned the switch off. And closed the drawer.

His real estate agent came in from the kitchen. "They're going to be here any minute. Is everything ready? Did you clean all the trash out of the closet? They are going to want to see inside."

"Why do they want to see my stuff? It's none of their business."

The agent sighed, "They don't care about your 'stuff'. They want to see how big the closet is, and having it packed full of clutter does not give the impression of boundless space. Did you hang up the clothes I gave you? It should look less than half full."

"Yah. I packed everything into boxes. It's still my house, you know."

Rolling his eyes, "If you want to sell it to them today, then you'll have to pack everything anyway. Think of it as an early start. Just let me do all the talking."

The doorbell put an end to their discussion.

The agent forced an exaggerated smile on his face as he opened the door. "Mr. Dursley, Ms. Dursley, please come in. You look so lovely today."

The couple that entered looked like they had stepped from an old photograph, where you had to hold still for a long time to get a clear image. He couldn't imagine either of them ever smiling. The man was dressed in a starched white shirt, jacket, and bow tie. He had a thin mustache and even thinner hair. The woman's blouse buttoned up to a tight collar with a brooch at her neck. She stood as if there were a metal rod running down her spine. Her lips were thin and pale in a tight line.

"We're here to see the house."

The agent did not let his smile falter. "Yes, of course. I'm so glad that you've come to see the property. Let me show you the kitchen." The tour continued as they went from room to room. The woman seemed intent on peering into every nook and corner, looking for dust or signs of mice.

When they were done, Mr Dursley turned to the agent. "The house matches the pictures you sent, but you were a little vague in the disclosure section of the agreement."

The agent's forehead was shiny with sweat now, and even his smile faltered. "Yes, well as you can see, it's a wonderful house, very well preserved, but there are some stories about it in the community. It's sort of a landmark. Famous, you might say."

Mr. Dursley frowned. "What sort of stories? What do you mean?"

The agent had to wipe his brow now. "Well, the house has been here for a long time, and local legends kind of grow up and get exaggerated over the years. Some people say that the house is…

haunted, or something like that. You know how people gossip."

Now, Ms. Dursley was looking wide-eyed and clutching at her collar as if she were wearing pearls. "You don't mean that someone was killed here!"

"No, no, no. Nothing like that. Nothing Untoward. There's a story that a ghost lives in the house." The agent was trying so hard to preserve his smile, but it was faltering.

Both of the Dursleys turned to look at the large TV in the room.

The agent spoke quickly. "It's nothing like that. It's not like in the movie."

Ms. Dursley looked at him suspiciously. "It's not in the TV?"

He tried to take a light, breezy air. "It moves around wherever it wants to. Sometimes it says hello from time to time. It's not any kind of issue. We have to include these things in the disclosure even when they have no real bearing on the market value of the property. It's a rule."

"He's very friendly and does his part of the housework." That earned him a glare from the agent.

Mr. Dursley seemed to acknowledge him for the first time. "Do you see ghosts?" He said this like it might be catchy, like a cold. Dursley looked at him suspiciously as they stepped back.

"You can't see him. He's just, you know." waving his arm vaguely about, motioning to a random part of the room. "He's very neat and tidy." Trying to think of something nice to say.

Mr Dursley stared at him. "You're saying that there is a ghost here with us right now?"

This must be how they look at crazy people. He was about to defend himself when there was an insistent beeping from the coffee table.

The agent looked up at the ceiling pleadingly.

Opening the drawer, he took out the Speak & Spell, putting it in the center of the table.

"Hello!"

"I am very pleased!"

"To meet you!"

Dursley was angry now. "What kind of charade is this? Do you think anyone will pay more money for a trick like this? What kind of scam are you trying to perpetrate here?"

"**No scam!**"

"**I hope that!**"

"**You will be!**"

"**Very happy here!**"

Mr Dursley was building up into a fine rage. "You programmed that!" As he pointed towards the toy with an accusing finger.

"**No program!**"

"**Better than!**"

"**Ouija board!**"

Ms. Dursley cried out, "Your house is possessed by demons!"

"He's not a demon." Under his breath, "Just a pain in my ass."

"**Here!**"

As a Kleenex floated through the air to Ms Dursley.

She screamed and ran from the room. As it turned out, her random flight took her into the kitchen. They all heard the familiar rapping on the refrigerator door followed by the scraping sound of the plastic letters rearranging themselves…

* * *

They watched the car's tires spin as it accelerated away from the house.

"I really thought they might have been the ones."

Behind them, they heard the Speak & Spell.

"Close door!"

"Close door!"

"Electric bill!"

Frank by Todd Brady de Garcia

It probably would have been better if I had been given a scarier name, right from the beginning, or if, at the very least, I hadn't had to wear reading glasses when I was already a not-like-anyone-else-kid, because no gone-to-school-for-the-first-time Sasquatch thinks it's funny hearing someone yell "Hey four eyes, Frank! Where are you off-to in such a hurry your Holy Furriness? Got a plane to catch? Let me guess; visiting your Great Aunt Hairball on "too-big-and-too-ugly for anyone" island again?"

Frank. Who names their baby Sasquatch "Frank?" My parent's should have known better. Way better. There has never, in the history of every Sasquatch throughout all of Sasquatch history, been a Sasquatch named Frank, that everyone didn't automatically laugh at. "Furry feet Frank", "Franky fuzzbutt", "Emptied the whole store of every single bottle of hair conditioner and still, just lookatcha all covered with split ends again. That must really suck", or, if they were in too much of a hurry and had no imagination, just leaving it at "Freak!"

So what. It would have sucked way worse to have stuck around for any more of their gunk; left town and everyone behind, like anyone with half-a-brain would have done, and renamed myself "Vamoose." Truthfully, everything was better without any of 'em around. Why bother with all of those whiny, bald-bodied-pink-people anyway. Who cares what they say when every last one of 'em was born boring; poor creatures. No wonder they always resort to pulling down whatever's around them; classic inadequacy.

Big words for some Sasquatch named Frank, who didn't even get past the first grade, I know. A Sasquatch with some vocabulary; just when you'd thought that I couldn't be scarier; joke's on you. Who knows what I'm capable of saying. It could be anything! It might even be something that you don't want to hear; something about you! Then, saying that whatever-it-is-thing, while pulling a giant tree up from the roots (which I would never do 'cause these giant trees are my true buddies) and then throwing it at you, or at whatever, just throwing it while spouting-off some unintelligible growly-stuff for sure gets 'em all runnin' away. People, for real; buncha loud-mouthed squat-bodied wussies; talk real big and run. I can tell that's all still true, even from three hundred football fields away; even with my glasses off.

And... there's the problem. Football.

This,there-ain't-no-such-thing, Sasquatch just happens to love football.

Talk about being a natural; just look at me. I'm made for it. Out there in the woods, among my beautiful community of giant-tree-BFFs, y'oughta see how clean and how far I can throw anyone's lost book bag. Never mind the town-talk about not believing that there's really any such thing as a Sasquatch, you'd have a much tougher time believing the clean, sweet distance I can get out of a book bag. Of course, a very important detail to remember, in order to keep that sailing-through-the-sky bookbag lookin' all pretty and sleek, is making sureI have added the right amount of heft to it. Too much gravity packed inside and the ground will start eye- balling it all hungry-like; reclaiming that football-bookbag from up high in the sky way too soon. Not enough stuff stuffed into the same bag, prior to launch, and just forget it. You'd hope that no one would ever see you trying to throw a weightless book bag without enough of anything in it. There'd be a whole new round of nicknames for me if I ever tried to do that. Good thing it's just me practicing with all of my tree buddies, who always take me exactly the right amount of seriously-enough, just like I do with them.

We're lucky like that together.

Here's the deal, though. Do you really think that this lumbering, ten-foot-tall emptied-out vacuum-bag of two-hundred year old furballs is gonna just huck a properly weighted book bag as far as it'll go without actually sitting down and reading all of the books that are in it first? I mean, c'mon, great personality for a furball or not, figure that part out, at least. You can talk to the trees for awhile, but eventually there's gotta be just a little bit more input. Am-I-right? Of course I am; and there ain't no library-people that'r gonna do anything but flip out if they see me comin' in, asking them where the short-fiction section is. So yeah, stolen book bags, in case you'd ever spent any time wondering how a mostly invisible 10-foot-tall Sasquatch could ever learn squat about squat, now you know. Reading. The next time your parents yell at you for losing another book bag, know that you can legit blame your friendly neighborhood Sasquatch; me.

One of these days I'll get to put down these perfectly-weighted book bags, at last, and play football for real, like on a team and stuff. I can picture the whole thing in my mind; a perfect day. On that one, perfect day, none of those super cute cheerleaders with their teeny-tiny skirts and giant pompoms will immediately start screaming at the top of their lungs the second they see the tiniest whisper of my shadow-shape (truly, I'm just watching the game) from deep within my group of comfortable trees right next to the football stadium, causing all of their 151-proof testosterone'd boyfriends, who are already begging for any reason to prove their gorilla'd-manliness, born ready to take on anything; now beating their chests and yelling "C'mon!"; the whole gang of linebackers headed straight for me, every single one of 'em hoping that their favorite winking-cheerleader is watching 'em, their sheer bravery hopefully making it a tiny bit more likely that they'd be rewarded with some tail for all of their huffing and puffing. Yeah, none of that stuff happens onmy perfect day.

Getting to actually play football, with a real football, on a true football team for the first time, right in front of everybody; that's what needs to pretty-please happen someday.

That day will be truly glorious. At the end of the game, when we've won a million to zero, 'cause of course, just look at me, really, and they're all asking me how I ever learned to play football like that while they all spray-laugh about not even being able to lift me up over their heads and group-cheer-yell together for our incredible victory, because again, I'm a ten-foot-tall 400-pound furball with hands, feet, and teeth; you ain't gonna be lifting me up. So, we all just keep on laughing and cheering and slappingeach other on the back (gently; remember, gently) so completely full of nothing but pure, unalloyed friendship exuberance and, wait… did one of those cheerleaders just wink at me too? See. It's all gonna happen just like I imagined.

Until then, thanks for all of the book bags

Frank

Rachel's Elevator

by Marshall Jared McAuley

Casey was a few months away from her sixteenth birthday the first time she saw the ghost. It wasn't like a movie - there was no tense music, no sound of screeching nails, no jump scares. Just a normal moment, like finding a wild animal staring back at you, both of you frozen in that space between fight or flight, waiting to see who flinches first. The fear came after, along with the overwhelming sound of her own heart, trying to smash its way out of her chest in a flood of adrenaline.

Excitement had been in short supply for Casey as the slow rhythm of summer ended and high school ramped up again. The frantic last-minute preparations and brief moments of fun seeing old friends before the grind of notes, projects, and activities set in almost felt normal. Or would have been if Casey herself felt normal. Instead, her summer had ended after the climbing incident in a blur of doctor visits, tests, and intense conversations with her parents.

She didn't do anything to deserve this, she often thought. She was careful not to overextend to the next hold, or stay on the wall too long, or climb higher than her ability to descend. She took the beginner or intermediate lines (problems" her climbing instructor had once called them) and felt fine after the session was over. Not like her older brother, who went after the routes like he had something to prove, leaving the callous on his hand torn and bleeding. But it was Casey who woke up that night, her arm and shoulder in so much pain that she lay gasping and twisting, wondering what was happening.

The pain had started in her arm, and at first it seemed like she had indeed overdone it at the climbing gym but after a few days it spread to her calf, her thigh, her shoulder and ribs. Most of her major muscles began to act like she had abused them, like walking downstairs to get a snack was the same exertion as running the suicide drills that used to be her favorite soccer practice.

Casey's friend Holly mocked her on the first day of school when she saw her arm in a sling. "What is it this time?" Holly laughed. Smaller than most of her friends and her brother on the playground, she had made up for her size with an overwhelming aggression in moments the other children least expected. It often got her into trouble. At eight, she punched a boy five years older than her just because she thought he was being mean to her friend.

She had started her freshman year of high school with her leg in a brace after knee surgery, the gift of an overenthusiastic lunge at a soccer ball in the tense final moments of a game. A blonde girl on the opposing team made a midget joke and Casey saw red. It was her trademark, the thing all her friends and family knew, that willingness to throw it all on the line when she was mad. Her mother loved to quote Shakespeare when they laughed about it - "Though she be but little, she is fierce."

Casey didn't feel particularly fierce as she made her way up the stairs in the academic hall, clutching the railing and gritting her teeth at the pain in her leg. Tenth grade was supposed to be better, she thought. She was no longer a new freshman to the looming three grades of older teens. This was supposed to be the start of her real "high school experience." Instead, here she was again, struggling to even navigate the long stairs in a building that felt more and more like a prison. She dodged one kid, climbing the stairwell like it was theirs alone - careless unless the person they clipped was bigger than them. She missed the second one in the press of anxious hurried bodies, and he bumped into her backpack with enough force to dislodge her death grip on the rail. She used her other hand to grab the metal and leaned away, barely catching herself. That will hurt tomorrow, she thought. The skinny kid who nudged her didn't even look, not registering that he had nearly knocked her down. "Asshole," Casey said under her breath, but it was lost in the din. She hated the passing period.

While changing classes was hellish, at least she was anonymous. Robert E. Lee High was a big school, nearing three thousand students, all pressing against its crumbling walls and decrepit paint. In the corridors and open spaces, it was easy to lose yourself, to just be a fish moving on the edge of the reef. It was when the bell was ringing, loud and obnoxious enough to be heard at her house a half mile away, and she was limping into class late that she hated more. It was then that she got the looks, those brief moments of caustic teenage judgement, the real currency of high school, and all she wanted was to crawl away and vanish. Some looks were indifferent, some curious, some sneering at the late arrival, but she hated all of them for noticing. She imagined they were the herd sensing the weak, the sick, the crippled member who would be left behind at the first sign of a predator.

Casey finally made it to her desk, in relief, and dropped a bag that felt heavier and heavier by the day. It thumped with a sound that might have included her Chromebook hitting the ground harder than recommended. She tried to breathe through the pain and rubbed her leg under the desk like the physical therapist had shown her. She attempted to focus on what the teacher was saying. He had launched into an explanation of acids and bases, but Casey immediately felt lost. Chemistry was hard on her best days, but she had missed school several times that week due to doctors' visits and early morning blood tests. After a few minutes trying to follow along, she gave up and her mind wandered. She wished again she knew what was wrong with her, that the tests had been conclusive, that she knew what to expect next. Instead, she was getting worse every week. I'm going to need crutches soon. She grimaced at the thought.

A long fifty minutes later and it was time to face the hall again. Third period passing was a little better as Mr. Davis's journalism class was just a few doors away in E Hall and didn't require braving the stairs. Better yet, the class was smaller, and most students just dove into their story assignments or media editing. They didn't look up as Casey limped in right as the bell announced its rigid adherence to the school clock.

Casey put her earbuds in and started editing. Mr. Davis paired students up and usually one would write the story, and the other would do the companion media, usually photos for the monthly paper, or a video essay for the school website . Casey hadn't been feeling well enough to do a feature story, so she was doing a video to accompany another student's story. A cell phone ban was being considered by the school board and passions on the topic ran high in the student body, giving her lots of juicy interviews to mold around the voice over track. Casey lost herself for a precious hour, trying different options and re-watching cuts until they seemed just right. She felt a hand on her shoulder and looked up as Mr. Davis gestured to take out the earbuds.

"You can leave class early to make it to the next period." Casey had completely lost track of time. She nodded absently at her teacher but the sudden return to reality from her flow state left a bitter taste and she muttered, "Lot of good it will do."

She regretted her words immediately, as Mr. Davis turned back to her with a concerned look. He was one of her better teachers, but Casey thought his best quality was that he left his students alone when they didn't need something, actually expecting them to get the work done on deadline with only the occasional feedback about journalistic objectivity. Now she had drawn his attention and prompted the thing she despised the most these days, sympathy.

Mr. Davis just looked at her, letting the obvious inquiry hang longer and longer, growing until it was unbearably heavy with social expectation. He was also patient. Finally, Casey blurted, "The stairs suck with my leg right now and the A Hall elevator is really far." Understanding bloomed on his face, "Ah. Right. Well, there is a service elevator at the back of E Hall. It's much closer than the main elevator."

"Really?" She was surprised. After starting her freshman year in a leg brace and fighting every day to shuttle between classes, trying to find the little used routes with the fewest people, she thought she knew the school. "The nurse and school counselor never mentioned it." What the hell, that would have made things way easier, she didn't say out loud.

Perceptiveness was another of Mr. Davis's qualities and he caught the disgruntled look. "It doesn't get used much these days, so they probably forgot. They built a door in front of it a few years ago and used the lobby as a janitor's closet. I use it occasionally to bring camera gear up. I've got a key that you can borrow."

Casey stood in the hall with Mr. Davis as he fiddled with the door to the janitor's closet. Casey shifted uncomfortably as other students moved past, feeling like she was being called into the principal's office. Mr. Davis got it unlocked and turned back to her, "The lock is a little temperamental, but the elevator is in the back." A student in the hallway called out to Mr. Davis and he turned, then remembered Casey and reached back to drop the key in her reluctant palm. "I'll get another from the janitor, so use this one as long as you need." Then he was gone.

Casey looked around the room and for a brief moment thought Mr. Davis had tricked her, as there were the large trashcans, buckets, mops, and the floor polishing machine you would expect in a school closet but seemingly nothing else. Then she caught a glimpse of the elevator door in the back corner, like a sinister black metal window.

As she worked her way slowly over to it, Casey noticed how out of place the elevator seemed. Up close, it was much older than the rest of the room, maybe original to the hundred year old building. There was a metal gate across the door, with diamond shaped openings giving a glimpse below of an old wooden platform and black beams in a confusing mess. As she looked up, she could see the pulleys and cables holding the elevator. There was a simple brass panel on the wall beside the gate with a round brass button sticking out. The space behind the gate was dark, the light from the window to the side not seeming to reach all the way back.

"You gotta be kidding me. Nope, nope, nope." Casey abruptly turned back towards the closet door, but knocked her leg into a bucket heavy with water. Growling at the pain, she made it to the door and paused, her hand on the knob. She could hear a group of students passing outside the door, chattering to each other. "Dammit. It probably won't even work."

Making a sudden decision, she limped back to the elevator and jammed her finger into the button. Surprisingly, there was an immediate grinding of gears from high above her and a single light turned on in the elevator shaft, lighting up the cables and a square metal shape moving up towards her from below. It came even with her and then passed, stopping abruptly. A faint ding sounded from somewhere in the darkness. After a few blank moments of silence, Casey realized that nothing else was going to happen. A handle caught her eye and, testing a theory, she grabbed hold of it and pulled. The diamond shapes collapsed as the gate accordioned to her left, revealing another door behind.

"That's messed up. You could totally lose a finger in that thing." Shaking her head and wondering how civilization survived to this point, Casey opened the door. Inside there was a worn wooden railing around a tiny room with grey industrial paint peeling, but otherwise it looked like…an elevator. She took a deep breath and pulled her bag further up her shoulder. Fine. Whatever. Can't believe I'm doing this.

Inside, she closed the gate first, then the door and examined the panel of four faded round buttons. Why are there four? The school only has three floors that she knew of. A moment later, she pursed her lips - a basement? A brief moment of curiosity spiked her thoughts, until she imagined a dark industrial basement, pipes and steam escaping as an axe murdering janitor lunged from the shadows. Hell. No.

A quick selection of the number one button and the rest of Casey's ride was uneventful, besides the sound of grinding gears and the sudden jerk at the start and stop of the trip. As she left the elevator, that first time, faintly surprised and distracted to have survived, she thought she heard a faint nondistinct voice coming from above. It was only a whisper of sound but vaguely familiar, like hearing the voice of her mother or brother upstairs and Casey responded without thinking. "What?" she called out and immediately felt foolish. It must have been someone else entering the closet room above her. She left the elevator quickly, wanting to avoid running into anyone else.

Over the next several weeks, the elevator became a lifeline. The physical relief from the pain of climbing the stairs, navigating the press of bodies, and having a few brief moments of solitude were like gravity, drawing her back until it became a daily ritual. Pulling the gate aside, the feel of the heavy old buttons that had to be pressed just right, the creaks and moans, the old gears and cables slipping and grinding all started to feel like the muttering of a grumpy old friend. She wondered, later, if that was why she started talking to it. "Cmon, I pushed your stupid button three times, now you finally feel like working?" "What are you complaining about, it's not like you have to do geometry, all you have to do is go up and down." "What was that wobble, you almost knocked me down?!" "How are you feeling today?" Groan, hiss. "Yeah, me too."

The next day, Casey couldn't walk. The muscles of her legs had locked up the night before while she was playing video games on the couch and her dad had to carry her to bed. More doctor visits and finally one morning she was shoved into a large machine that clanged away loudly at her and took pictures of the inside of her muscles, showing the deterioration she could already feel.

Her dad taped small towels to the armpit cushions on her crutches, which helped the chafing a little, but only added to the stares of others when she returned to school a week later. I don't know how much longer I can do this, she thought as she awkwardly pushed her way into the elevator closet, swinging the crutches around to let the door close behind her. Withdrawn and quiet while she called the elevator, Casey contemplated what being in a wheelchair would feel like.

On the brief ride down, Casey was distracted enough that it took her a moment to register that the elevator had stopped. Slowing down or lurching was nothing new as the cable sliding on the pulley hit its worn spots, but it had never stopped before. "You've got to be kidding—" The words froze in her throat. A shadowed face was in the corner of the elevator, dark against the light.

As anyone would, she at first thought it was a trick of the shadow and looked up to see what was blocking the weak ceiling light, but there was nothing. Her eyes darted back down, and the face was still there, maybe not a momentary imagination. Moreover, she realized with a jolt, the face was looking back at her. Shadows don't have eyes, she thought. This one did. As she stared at it, she could somehow feel it notice her look and focus on her, realizing she could see it, realizing that each was aware of the other.

Casey's heart spasmed into action, beating a wild rhythm, and she could feel the rush of warmth in her chest, the backs of her hands, and in her mouth, suddenly dry with something she recognized from watching her brother play horror games. Fear.

It was a long moment, the tension stretching, until Casey realized that the face was also quivering and recognized the reflection of her own frozen state in the dark, indistinct features. She managed to work enough saliva into her mouth to whisper "Wh…who…," and it was gone, never there, and the elevator ground back into action. "…are you?" she finished as the descent ended and the ancient bell dinged weakly.

Sitting stunned in her next class, Casey ignored the teacher's drone and hunched down over her Chromebook. A Google search claimed that, while many people over the centuries reported seeing ghosts, there was no empirical proof, no evidence whatsoever after the alleged sightings, visitations, and mystical experiences. The investigations all produced nothing. There was even a definition that made her wince back from the laptop screen, pareidolia - the tendency of human brains to see patterns in random noise. Faces in clouds, figures in the shadows.

The next day, in her journalism class the discussion turned to planning the upcoming October issue of the school paper. Halloween traditions, the best places to trick or treat, which neighborhoods to avoid. When the conversation turned to a classmate's passionate defense of Swedish Fish as the best Halloween candy, Casey's hand crept up, almost of its own accord. Mr. Davis cut the other student off and gestured for Casey's question.

"Are there any ghosts in the school?"

That set the group off and produced a rapid fire of school legends. A senior claimed to know a kid who saw a weird mist in the courtyard once, a sophomore had heard about a "grey lady" at the nearby middle school, and another girl said in the thirties there was a lynching in the big oak tree by the annex building and the branches used in the hanging didn't move in the wind.

Mr. Davis shook his head at all of them, "You guys never heard of Rachel's grave?" A general murmur of dissent, but Casey's breath hitched with an echo of her earlier fear. Mr. Davis mused, "I probably shouldn't tell you this…"

He knew, as all teachers do, that forbidden knowledge to teenagers is like honey to a bee, irresistible. They pressed him to tell the story. Taking his time, Mr. Davis told them that a portion of the school building had been built on a Civil War graveyard and in the 80's, a renovation had uncovered a gravestone with a single name of 'Rachel' along with the inscription, 'Our Daughter, cut down but not destroyed.' Every few years since, a random student claimed to have seen a shape or a voice and somehow, they all knew they had seen Rachel.

Mr. Davis reflected, "There was even a group of students that made a short film about it, but that was before I got here. It's been at least 15 years since anyone saw her, so I guess I shouldn't be surprised none of you know the story."

Casey's voice cut across the class, "I'll write about her." An older student started to laugh before Mr. Davis shut them down with a raised eyebrow. He turned back to Casey, "Well, we hadn't decided on all the assignments... It is a good fit for the Halloween edition. Could be a feature, maybe front page, but it's a lot of work. Are you sure?"

Casey wanted to slink away from the question, from the looks of her classmates all turned towards her now, but something held her back. Her mind whirled, for the thousandth time thinking of the elevator and those black, shadow eyes looking back at her, seeing her. She hadn't slept well the night before. What was it? She had to know. Face burning, she nodded sharply to Mr. Davis, "I'll do it."

Casey started the story the way she always did — hoping to lose herself in the work — but the elevator kept bleeding through the edges of her thoughts. The grinding gears. The shadowed face. The single name Mr. Davis had dropped into class like bait. *Rachel.*

Her browser search history grew increasingly irritated: *Rachel Robert E. Lee High ghost. Grave found during renovation. Civil War cemetery school. Why won't you tell me what I need? Why is Google shitty?* After a few days of dead ends, and at Mr. Davis's suggestion, she gave up on her laptop and trudged into the library.

The librarian had nearly cackled, wheeling out the ancient machine from a closet. Casey shook her head as it was set on the table. "God, this belongs in a museum." After a five-minute tutorial, the microfilm reader whirred softly, projecting shaky headlines and grainy photographs like some low-budget time machine.

Most of it was lame — zoning meetings, sports scores, PTA bickering. Then she found it. A filler story tucked into the local section: *Construction crew uncovers grave during high school renovations.* The photo was small and blurry, but the headstone was clear enough: *Rachel. Our daughter. Cut down but not destroyed.*

Casey traced the words with her finger, feeling the same prickling awareness she had in the elevator. The article didn't mention a last name. No dates, no family, no story. Just Rachel, and the headstone that marked her as someone who had once lived and died, then been erased except for those eight stubborn words.

And the elevator? The photo made her stomach tighten. The workers were standing right where the janitor's closet would be now.

The next time she took the elevator, she couldn't pretend it was just about avoiding the stairs. She waited with her palms damp, her body tense, as the elevator groaned into motion, the cables thrumming faintly in the shaft. Casey leaned on the wooden rail, her bag heavy on her shoulder. The elevator finished its trip, but she didn't move. She looked at the shadows. "Really? Nothing?" She sighed and was about to leave when she felt a change in the air. Cold. Heavy. The light flickered.

At first it was only a distortion in the corner, a ripple in the shadows like heat rising from asphalt. Then the face again, darker this time, more defined. Eyes that shouldn't exist watching her, unblinking.

Casey's throat tightened but she forced the words out. "Rachel? Is that you?"

The shape quivered, almost like it wanted to answer. Her heart hammered so hard she thought the elevator itself could hear it. "What happened to you? What do you want?"

The air pressed in, thick and heavy, a pressure building in her ears. Then—

nothing. The shape folded into the darkness as though it had never been there. The elevator dinged faintly, reminding her to get off. Casey staggered out, her mouth dry, furious at the silence.

Another fitful, sleepless night, another day of fidgeting through classes and Casey was in front of the elevator again. She stumbled her crutches into it and held her breath as it descended but this time there was nothing. She rode it four times that day, going out of her way between classes to ride, fists clenched with frustration. She only stopped when she was five minutes late to English. She almost didn't care this time about the looks and the snickers - the girl on crutches interrupting class. Almost.

Over the next week, she distracted herself with research for the story. Her elevator trips were uneventful and after a few days she began to doubt. Doubt what she had seen, doubt what she had felt, doubt her sanity. Nothing seemed certain.

Casey's body continued to fail her. Her arms were inflamed from putting weight on the crutches and she stopped being able to go to school. More doctors, new doctors, further away. Sleepy car rides in the morning to get blood tests before she ate or drank anything. Waiting.

One morning, a long call from the new doctor. *Polymyositis*. Her immune system was eating her own muscles. Months, maybe years, of immunosuppressor treatments. No soccer, no climbing, no running stairs two at a time.

The infusion room at the hospital smelled like antiseptic and plastic tubing. Casey stared at the IV line snaking into her arm, the cold trickle of medication seeping into her body. Her mom sat beside her, pretending to read a magazine but glancing up every few minutes with the same fragile look. "I'm fine, Mom" she answered the unspoken question.

Casey turned her face away from the magazine pages her mom kept shifting. She didn't want sympathy. She wanted answers. In the silence between the beeping of machines, her mind went back to Rachel, to the headstone, to the shadow that almost spoke.

At least they let her have her Chromebook in the room, although she had to type one handed. She hated how slow it made her. Tap, tap, tap. Her story was almost done. She had described how the graves were found, how most were crushed, broken, and illegible before the crew realized what they were. She wrote of Rachel's single name and the epitaph engraved in defiance of her death. The stone had caught the imagination of the whole town for a time and they debated what to do with it but in the end decided to keep it as close to where it was found as possible. In the years since, the sightings, the rumor's, the gleefully overwrought stories of the ghost then, nothing. Tales of Rachel faded another footnote in the dustbin of history.

Casey shifted, trying to get comfortable, a little hard to do with the needle and the medical tape starting to irritate the skin of her arm. That part about the grave bothered her - it was creepy that the headstone was still there in the school basement, underneath all the students walking the halls every day, a reminder of how illness and death comes, even for the young. She dreamed often of the basement.

Returning to school after weeks away was like walking into back into a movie that had kept going without her. The faces were the same, but everything felt just a little too fast, too loud, too bright. The fluorescent lights buzzed like they were mocking her, the rush of students in the hallways a current she couldn't step into.

Casey didn't stop at her class. She kept walking, crutches clattering faintly, the sound sharp against the tile. Down the quieter stretch of A Hall, where the old lockers were half-rusted and the ceiling tiles sagged with water stains, she found the janitor's door.

Her palms were slick when she turned the knob.

Inside, the closet was dim, the smell of cleaner and dust thick in her throat. She shut the door behind her and just stood for a moment, the silence pressing close, her breath echoing faintly. Then she turned toward the elevator.

She stared for a long minute at the lowest button — *Basement.*

Inside the elevator, the button felt colder than she remembered. When she pressed it, the gears above groaned to life, louder and slower than before, a grind that reverberated through her ribs. The elevator shook, then settled with a heavy thud that made her teeth ache. The ceiling light flickered once, then twice, then steadied into a weak yellow glow.

Casey swallowed hard.

The air that hit her when she opened the gate was stale and damp, and she felt it cling to her skin like cobwebs. The smell of mildew was stronger here — old water and rust and something faintly metallic. She stepped forward, crutches tapping softly on the concrete, her shadow stretching ahead of her into the gloom.

The basement was bigger than she'd imagined, a long corridor broken by thick stone pillars. The walls were raw and uneven, veins of mortar showing through. Pipes ran overhead, black and sweating, and she could hear the slow drip of water somewhere out of sight.

No steam, no axe-murdering janitor, she told herself, but even in her own head the attempt at humor fell flat against the thick silence.

She made her way toward the far corner, her steps echoing. And then she saw it — the headstone, small and half-buried in dust, sitting beneath a single bare bulb. A historical plaque, itself faded, was on the wall by the stone. The light cast it in a lonely circle of gold. *Rachel. Our daughter. Cut down but not destroyed.*

Casey's fingers tightened around the crutch handle until her knuckles went white. The rest of the basement seemed to lean inward — the darkness pooling in the corners, the faint hum of the building above fading away.

"Okay," she whispered, her voice sounding too loud in the still air. "I'm here."

Nothing.

Her heartbeat filled the silence.

"I know you're here," she said again, louder. "Why me? Why show yourself to me?"

The shadows shifted — not like something moving in the light, but like the dark itself had drawn breath. A chill rolled across her skin.

She swallowed. "I'm sick," she said, her words catching. "My body's attacking itself. I spend more time in hospitals than with my friends." Her voice cracked. "Do you know what that's like? To feel like you're disappearing?"

For a moment, the shadows just trembled, like the air before a storm. Then she saw it — the faint outline of a girl, thinner than smoke, barely a shimmer in the dark. Her arm lifted, slow and hesitant, reaching toward Casey.

Casey didn't move. Her heart thudded in her throat, but under the fear came something else again — recognition. A thought rose unbidden, sharp and certain.

"That's it," she breathed. "You were disappearing. We were forgetting about you."

The figure seemed to pause, her shape wavering as if a gust of wind passed through her. The light bulb flickered once, twice. For a heartbeat, Casey thought she saw a face — young, tired, sad — and then it was gone.

The bulb steadied. The basement was still.

Casey let out a breath she hadn't realized she'd been holding. The air was thin again, ordinary and stale, but her pulse had slowed. She leaned on her crutch, staring at the stone.

"Not anymore," she said softly.

And then she turned, the echo of her steps following her back to the elevator, the darkness settling behind her like a closing hand.

Casey's story came out in the October edition of the school paper: *Rachel's Ghost: The Hidden History of Robert E. Lee High.* Seeing her own name in the byline felt strange — like it belonged to someone braver, someone who hadn't spent the last two months limping through the hallways and hiding from attention.

Mr. Davis called it a solid feature, "a little melodramatic," but good work. Her friend Holly said she read it twice, though Casey couldn't tell if that was admiration or gaslighting. A few students in other classes asked questions, their voices hushed, half-teasing, half-curious. For once, Casey didn't mind being noticed.

That afternoon, she left journalism without glancing toward the janitor's door. The elevator waited somewhere behind it, silent, patient, part of its own story now. Casey's legs still ached, but the infusions were finally helping. For the first time in months, she chose the stairs. She hesitated at the top, the metal rail cool beneath her fingers, and then started down.

Halfway to the landing, a boy came barreling past, shoving her shoulder hard enough that she staggered. Her crutch slipped for a heartbeat, and the world tilted.

Instinct surged before fear could smother it.

"Hey, shithead!" Her voice cracked like a whip through the stairwell. Heads turned. People noticed — not with pity, but surprise. The boy stopped, blinking, mumbled an awkward, "Sorry," before hurrying on.

Casey tightened her grip on the railing, steadying herself. Her heart raced — but it wasn't the wild panic of before. It was something else, something sharper. For the first time in a long time, she felt almost fierce again.

www.ingramcontent.com/pod-product-compliance
Lightning Source LLC
Chambersburg PA
CBHW071221260626
47162CB00004B/1389